The Ghost Train

Written by ANDREW CHARMAN

Illustrated by SUE DEAKIN

Derrydale Books

New York/Avenel, New Jersey

A TEMPLAR BOOK

This 1992 edition published by Derrydale Books,
distributed by Outlet Book Company, Inc., a Random House Company,
40 Engelhard Avenue, Avenel, New Jersey 07001.

First published in Canada in 1992 by Smithbooks,
113 Merton Street, Toronto, Canada M45 1AB.

Devised and produced by The Templar Company plc,
Pippbrook Mill, London Road, Dorking, Surrey RH4 1JE, Great Britain.

Edited by A J Wood
Designed by Janie Louise Hunt
Printed and bound in Singapore

ISBN 0-517-06972-5
8 7 6 5 4 3 2 1

P agan Place was a tall, dark house that stood on a hill at the edge of town. It could be seen for miles around and all the people of the town were scared of going near it.

Sam's grandmother said that when she was young, an old woman by the name of Mrs Crablook had lived there. She wore long black dresses in the style of a hundred years before, she never went out, and everyone, even the grown-ups, was frightened of her. After the old lady's death, the house had been put up for sale. But no one came to look at it; no one dared to.

Over the years, Pagan Place fell slowly into a state of decay. The hinges on the doors rusted solid, the brickwork crumbled, and all you could see through the windows was a cloud of cobwebs. The yard was choked with weeds, and the trees had become scraggly and twisted with age. Bats made their home in the roof, and they could be seen circling around the chimneys at dusk. People who were brave enough to pass by the house at night said that they had heard

strange noises coming from inside, and some even reported seeing faces at the windows.

When Sam, Billy, and Clara were outside in the street, they were always aware of Pagan Place. In the dark shadows of evening, the house seemed to grow and lean menacingly towards the town.

Billy's grandmother was always telling them that Pagan Place was haunted. But although they thought the house was spooky, not one of them really believed that ghosts lived there. Little did they know!

Inside the gloomy old house, at the end of the darkest passage you could ever imagine, there stood a door. It was shrouded by cobwebs and never opened.

Behind it was a room full of old furniture. The curtains hung in tatters at the windows and a thick layer of dust covered every object. Anyone entering this dark and dusty place on a sunny, autumn afternoon would have been surprised to hear the sound of a piano playing faintly somewhere in the stillness.

They would have been even more surprised to see a tall, unhappy-looking man standing in front of the room's gilded mirror. He was dressed in a black suit, with an old-fashioned wing-collar, and huge brown shoes. Taking a deep breath, he pulled his face into a grisly grimace and moaned:

"OOOOooooooohhhhhh!"

"Oh, come on, Herbert," said another man who was lounging on the moth-eaten sofa, dressed as a pirate captain. "You've been dead for fifty years. Surely you can look more scary than that?"

"Well, I'm sorry," replied Herbert in a gloomy voice. "I don't feel well and I'm out of practice. I'm doing my best."

"Look, watch me!" said the other ghost, and he leapt up, let out a blood-chilling scream and pulled off his head. Then he tucked it under his arm and danced around the room. "See! It's easy!" he laughed.

Just then, the ghost who had been playing the piano stepped forward and said in a very well-spoken voice:

"The problem, my dears, is that we don't have anyone to scare. It's all very well pulling faces in front of mirrors. What we need is real, living people to frighten." The others nodded.

Mr Fergusson was well-respected among the other ghosts. He had been dead for over 400 years and had come from England. He wore very old-fashioned clothes and had once had dinner with William Shakespeare. He turned to Mrs Crablook.

"What do you think, Madam?"

The old lady was busy knitting cobwebs in a dark corner. She made them for the spiders who were too old to make their own.

"I think we need to launch a campaign of terror," she said. "We're wasting our time in this house. No one comes here. We must leave the house and scare the wits out of the people in this town before we all forget how to do it."

With that, the old lady reached over and pulled a rope that hung by her side. The rope fell from the ceiling in a cloud of dust, bringing bits of plaster down with it. Deep in the recesses of the house, a bell rang. A moment later, in floated Clarence

the spirit, balancing a tray of tea things on one arm. Clarence was pale and wispy, a shapeless creature who flew everywhere.

"Over here," called Mrs Crablook. "Yes… er… thank you Clarence."

Clarence flew around the room, his cloud-like body curling around the ornaments and picture frames. The others tried to steady him, but he was out of control again. He floated up to the ceiling, circled three times around the light-fitting, and disappeared.

"Oh, dear," sighed Mrs Crablook. "Will someone please catch up with Clarence and fetch the tea things?"

Down at the bottom of the hill, the
townspeople were preparing for Halloween, the night
when ghosts haunt the living and witches fly through
the sky. Everyone was planning to dress up in a
Halloween costume. Sam, Billy, and Clara were busy
making their outfits and they were all excited. Sam put
on his monster mask and crept up behind Clara who
was busy finishing off her witch's cloak.

"Grrrrggghh," roared Sam. Clara let out a
scream and clutched her heart.

"If you do that once more," she shouted, putting on her tall, black hat and waving her wand at her brother, "I'll turn you into a frog." Sam hopped out of the room laughing and Clara followed, cackling behind him. But they both stopped suddenly in the hall and froze in horror at the sight of a pale, shapeless figure before them…

The spirit turned and raised its arms and moaned. They recognized the voice – it was Billy!

Throughout the town, excitement was growing. Witches cackled and whizzed here and there on broomsticks, monsters clomped and groaned up and down the street, and specters floated in and out of rooms. The next day was Halloween when there would be a street parade, a giant funfair, *and* a bonfire party.

The children were planning to be more scary than ever before. Sam, Billy, and Clara tried their disguises out on the family. Their grandmother was not impressed – she'd seen too many ghosts to be frightened of children in costumes. But Uncle Tom was so scared that he let go of his lawn mower which careered straight into the neighbor's pond. Their mother screamed and stepped back into the dog's food bowl, and Mrs Coleman from next door put her hands to her face, ran inside, and wasn't seen until the following Wednesday.

At Pagan Place, preparations were also underway. Mrs Crablook draped cobwebs over her ancient clothes. Herbert practiced his menacing faces and Clarence drifted through the eerie house making things go bump. In his room, the Captain pulled off his head and put it back on again several times until the action was quite smooth and unlikely to go wrong.

Meanwhile, Mr Fergusson found some spiders
who were happy to live in his beard and busied
himself by pressing his clothes. Soon, the ghostly
group was ready to give the town the fright of its life.
They had no idea that they had chosen to do their
spooking on the night of Halloween!

The night started well. A storm raged through the district accompanied by terrible thunder and long, forked fingers of lightning. Owls hooted somewhere in the darkness of the woods and spiders busily wove webs where there had never been webs before. The

ghosts of Pagan Place floated noiselessly through the doors and walls of their crumbling home and made for the town.

"I think we should spook this one first," said Mrs Crablook, pointing to one of the nearby houses.

Everyone nodded, and the Captain's head fell off. Herbert stood at the front door and knocked loudly and slowly three times. Clarence floated up to a bedroom window and peered in, while Mrs Crablook scratched her long fingernails against the downstairs windows.

Inside, the McTavish twins were expecting their friends to arrive at any moment. They were already wearing their Halloween costumes. Bob looked grisly as a green and yellow ghoul with huge boils on his neck. Geraldine wore a wig of rubber snakes that flopped and curled around her forehead.

"That will be the others," said Geraldine when she heard the knock at the door. "Come on, Bob! Let's give them a scare."

The two children flung open the door. Bob roared and dribbled from the corner of his mouth, and Geraldine shook her head and made the snakes wriggle and writhe. Herbert had never seen anything so frightening, not in life or death.

"H... H... Help!" he stammered, and he turned and fled. He ran past Mrs Crablook who was staring in horror at the monstrous creatures in the doorway. Mr Fergusson and the Captain were already heading for the street, running as fast as they could.

"Quick! Follow Herbert!" they shouted.

The twins were pleased with themselves.

"Wow!" said Bob. "We really scared them!"

"I've never seen Sam and Billy run so fast," laughed Geraldine. "Clara's costume looked great, didn't it?"

As they turned back into the house, Bob and Geraldine met Clarence in the hallway. Clarence floated up to the ceiling and moaned, "OOooooohhh."

Then he took one look at Bob, who at that moment was struggling to get out of his mask, gulped and sped through a wall.

"Bob, that was a real ghost," said Geraldine, excitedly. "It went through the wall!"

But Bob hadn't seen Clarence – he had been too busy trying to free himself from his mask.

"Nonsense," he said. "There's no such thing as a real ghost."

The inhabitants of Pagan Place were a long
way from their home by now and in a state of great
confusion. They ran down the main street of the town
in utter horror. Everywhere they turned they saw
ghosts, ghouls, monsters, and witches. At one point, a
demon with a forked tail and horns came up to the
Captain and shook his hand. The Captain's hand came
away at the wrist.

"Brilliant!" cried the demon appreciatively. "How do you do that?" The Captain didn't wait to answer – he picked up his hand and ran.

The ghosts were just passing the entrance to the funfair when Sam, Billy, and Clara appeared out of an alleyway in their Halloween costumes.

"L… L… Look!" stammered Herbert. "More of them." And, without looking where they were going, the ghosts blundered into the fairground to escape.

"Hey, wait for us," shouted Sam after the ghosts, and then turning to the others he said: "Come on, there must be something happening at the funfair. Be scary!"

So Clara and Billy followed Sam, laughing all the way. Up ahead, Herbert was paler than he'd ever been before, Mrs Crablook had lost most of her cobwebs, and Mr Fergusson, usually so smartly dressed, was looking shabby and red in the face.

"Quick! On the Ghost Train," cried Clarence, spotting a sign. "Perhaps we'll shake them off there." The ghosts passed through the walls of the Ghost Station and climbed on board the waiting train. It was silent inside. Then they heard a clacking sound.

"SSssshhh," said Mr Fergusson. "What's that noise?"

"It's m… m… my teeth," stammered Herbert. "I've never b… b… been on a g… ghost train before. I'm scared." And he took out his teeth and put them in his pocket to stop them chattering. Suddenly, the train gave a lurch, then a jolt, and started rolling forward.

"Hold on everyone," shouted Mr Fergusson.

The Ghost Train gathered speed and disappeared into the darkness of a tunnel. Suddenly, lights flashed and lit up ghoulish faces that leered and grinned out of the shadows. A bright, white skeleton leapt out of nowhere and dangled in front of them. Something wet hit Herbert in his left ear and a mechanical spider fell from the ceiling. The darkness

was filled with the sounds of groaning, moaning, creaking, and eerie laughing. Eventually, the train slowed down and stopped. Mrs Crablook looked at Mr Fergusson with surprise.

"Well, that wasn't very scary, was it?" she said.

"Did you see that specter?" asked Clarence. "It was rubbish. I could do better than that any day."

"I wasn't frightened either," said Herbert, opening his eyes for the first time.

Just then the ghosts heard the sound of voices and the train wobbled as people climbed on board.

"Oh, no!" cried Clarence. "It's those monsters again. Whatever shall we do?"

"But look!" cried Mr Fergusson, staring hard at the nearest passenger. "They're not monsters at all. They're children wearing silly costumes – and that has given me a *brilliant* idea!"

Quickly, he whispered a plan to the others.
They knew exactly what he had in mind.

The Captain unfastened the cardboard skeleton
and stood in its place. Mrs Crablook sat in a rocking
chair beside the rails and Mr Fergusson stood where
the lights would shine directly onto his elegant face.

The children on the Ghost Train had never had a better ride. They whooped and hollered and screamed as the train flashed through the darkness. They were terrified when they saw Mrs Crablook in her rocking chair scowling at them. The Captain horrified everyone by removing his head and spinning

it on his finger as if it were a basketball. Clarence
followed the train throughout, swooping in and out of
the carriages. But the best performance was Herbert's.
He stood in the middle of the tracks as the train
approached. All the passengers held their breath and
waited for him to step out of the way. But he didn't.

The Captain stepped onto the tracks as well.
The train roared straight through him and, as it sped
away, he turned and waved at the passengers. When
the children arrived back at the platform, they were
laughing and cheering.

"That's the best ghost train ever," laughed Sam.

"And you could see right through that old
lady. It was amazing!" said Billy.

"It was as if they were real ghosts," said Clara, excitedly. "Come on, let's go round again."

So they went round again, and again, and again until they were exhausted. The ghosts perfected their act. They had never been so scary, nor had so much fun. So they decided to stay for a little while.

"We can always go home again when it gets boring," suggested Mrs Crablook.

Over the months that followed, the Ghost Train became famous for miles around. Everyday, the carriages were packed with people who wanted to be scared out of their wits. They were never disappointed.

People who came again and again were surprised to find that the ride never seemed to be the same twice. The man who ran the Ghost Train kept it open all year round and made so much money that he eventually bought Pagan Place. For some reason it wasn't scary any more.

The ghosts heard about it one day, after a good spooking. But instead of being upset Mrs Crablook smiled at the others and said:

"You know, I don't think I want to go home after all. I'm just getting into the spirit of the thing!"